Annie Antelope

Dave and Pat Sargent are longtime residents of Prairie Grove, Arkansas. Dave, a fourth-generation dairy farmer, began writing in early December 1990, and Pat, a former teacher, began writing shortly after. They enjoy the outdoors and have a real love for animals.

Annie Antelope

By

Dave and Pat Sargent

Illustrated by
Jeane Huff

Ozark Publishing, Inc.
P.O. Box 228
Prairie Grove, AR 72753

Library of Congress Cataloging-in-Publication Data

Sargent, Dave, 1941—
     Annie Antelope / by Dave and Pat Sargent ;
   illustrated by Jeane Huff.
       p. cm.
       Summary: At bedtime, Annie Antelope wanders
   away from home and alomst becomes a meal for a
   timber wolf.
       ISBN 1-56763-358-7 (cb). — ISBN 1-56763-359-5
   (pb)
       [1. Pronghorn antelope—Fiction.   2.
   Wolves—Fiction. 3. Behavior—Fiction.]   I.
   Sargent, Pat, 1936—   . II. Huff, Jeane, 1946—ill.
   III. Title.
       PZ7.S2465An 1998
       97-27106
       [Fic]—dc21   CIP
                                                            AC

Printed in the United States of America

iv

Inspired by

watching young antelope run alongside their mamas. They move with ease and are so graceful.

Dedicated to

all children who, like our grand-daughters, love ballet.

Foreword

Annie is a young antelope who loves everyone and everything. She is an optimist. She thinks every wild animal wants to be her friend. She is surprised to learn that a great big ole timber wolf has his eye on her, not because he wants her for a friend, but because he hasn't eaten in several days and is so hungry!

Contents

Annie Antelope

If you would like to have the authors of the Animal Pride Series visit your school, free of charge, call 1-800-321-5671 or 1-800-960-3876.

One

Annie! Come Home!

"Annie! It's time for bed," Mama Antelope called. She waited, but Annie did not come. "Annie! Annie! Can you hear me, Annie?"

Annie's twin brother, Danny, said, "Annie ran down the hill, Mama. I told her you wouldn't want her to go that far, but she wouldn't listen. She just kept running. Did Annie run away from home, Mama? Did she?"

"Annie wouldn't do something like that. Annie is a happy girl,"

1

Mama Antelope said, smiling at Danny. "She knows we love her. She will come home soon."

Mama Antelope and Danny were busy eating the tender grass. They always swallowed first and chewed later. Since antelope have no biting teeth in the upper front jaw, Mama Antelope, Danny, and Annie always tore off the grass stems and swallowed without chewing. Later, they regurgitated the grass from their stomachs in small wads, or cuds, and chewed it well with their molars.

Mama was quiet for a moment, remembering the things Annie did, things like risking her life because she trusted other animals too much. It seemed to Annie's mama that Annie always put a little too much faith in others. Mama worried that one of those *trusted* animals would someday turn on her little girl.

Mama Antelope knew in her heart that Annie was an optimist because Annie believed in everyone and everything. She thought every antelope was a good antelope. She thought every coyote, every wolf, every bobcat, every black panther, every cougar, every animal on the face of the earth, wild or tame, would not hurt her if she was nice to it. And this worried Annie's mama. She was afraid that Annie was just a little too trusting. Mama Antelope was something of an optimist her-self, and she knew that being an optimist was a good thing. But Annie was, perhaps, a little too much of an optimist.

Suddenly Annie came sailing out of the trees and ran right smack-dab into Danny and Mama Antelope.

A coyote by the name of Cody had stopped at the edge of the woods and watched Annie run up close to her mama. Shucks! He was going to miss supper again. He had missed several suppers lately, and he was getting mighty hungry.

Cody stood with his big eyes glued to little Annie Antelope. He knew she would be good eating. If he could only get close enough, he could bring her down.

It was a good thing Annie's mama was standing beside young Annie. As long as Annie stayed close to her mama, she would be safe. Well, she would be much safer than she would be off by herself.

While Mama Antelope was watching the young coyote working his way back and forth, slipping up closer and closer to her little family, Annie turned and slipped away. When Mama looked back over her shoulder, she couldn't believe her eyes. Her little Annie was gone. Mama Antelope watched the coyote go slinking off into the woods and

wondered if he was going to pick up
Annie's scent.

Later that day, Annie came bounding into sight, looking all tired out but happy. Mama Antelope said, "Just look at her, Danny. That sister of yours doesn't seem to have a care in the world. She still believes that nothing bad can ever happen to her. Yes, little Annie is an optimist. Oh, well, it's good to be optimistic, Danny. Well, most of the time it's a good way to be."

The next morning, Annie took off again, out of sight of Danny and out of sight of her mama. There was no doubt about it, Annie was the adventuresome type. She knew she was supposed to stay close to her family until she was a little older and better able to take care of herself, but she didn't seem to remember these very important things. She thought nothing bad would ever happen to her.

Mama Antelope and Danny stood on top of the hill and gazed off down the side of it. There was no Annie in sight.

A soft blay now came from Mama Antelope. Suddenly, she felt afraid for her baby. It had been a long, hard winter. What if a hungry wolf or coyote had spotted Annie running down the hill by herself? Again, Mama Antelope blayed, this time, a little louder.

Down below and around a bend in the creek, Annie was running for her life. A huge gray timber wolf that had not eaten in more than a week was hot on her trail. Lobo had snatched a scent off the breeze that was blowing from Annie's direction. All he had to do was follow his nose. He was headed right toward the little antelope.

Annie was a young antelope, but somehow she knew that danger was near. She had an excellent nose, and a sudden shift in the wind had alerted her that a wild animal was close by. And without knowing that the wild animal was a hungry wolf, little Annie knew to run. And that's just what she was doing: the little antelope was running for her life. Poor Annie!

Up ahead, Annie Antelope saw a high wall of trees and bushes. She didn't know what to do. She was so afraid! She made a leap, trying to jump over the brush, but she was just too small, or her legs were too short. Whatever the reason, Annie's front feet got tangled up, and the poor little antelope fell headfirst into the brush.

A pitiful cry escaped Annie's throat. It rolled out through her open mouth and right up the hill to her mama.

Mama Antelope's ears perked up. They flicked forward. She heard Annie's desperate cry for help. In two seconds flat, Mama Antelope went bounding down the side of the hill, hoping against hope that she would be in time to save her little Annie.

Danny didn't move. He knew he couldn't run as fast as his mama, and if he followed, she would have two little babies to worry about. So Danny stayed on the hill, hoping that the wild animal, whatever it was, didn't pick up his scent and come after him, too.

Two

The Hungry Wolf

When Mama Antelope veered sharply to the right, following the riverbank, her eyes scanned the woods ahead. There was no sign of young Annie. She started to call out but checked herself. If little Annie was hidden, out of sight, she would be much safer if she remained quiet and didn't answer her mama's call.

Mama Antelope began leaping high into the air, first to the right, then to the left, her eyes searching for Annie.

When Annie Antelope's mama first caught sight of ole Lobo, her heart skipped several beats. Why, it almost stopped beating. This was the biggest timber wolf she had ever, in her entire life, laid eyes on! And then, Mama saw Annie. Annie was caught in the brush, all tangled up, unable to run from the wolf.

The timber wolf was crouched low, almost crawling on his stomach, inching closer and closer to Annie. Mama Antelope could see that ole wolf's mouth watering.

The wolf was so intent on catching and eating Annie that he was not aware of Annie's mama coming up on him. She was bounding high into the air, her feet hardly touching the ground. That wolf was totally unprepared for what was about to happen.

When Mama Antelope spotted the wolf, she had wheeled and run back along the river for a ways, then whirled around. And by the time she reached the wolf, she must have been going thirty-five miles an hour!

Mama Antelope whirled in midair and, with her strong back legs, kicked backward with all her might! Her hooves caught Lobo and sent him sailing! His body flew high into the air, then hit the ground with a thud. He lay there, unmoving.

Mama Antelope helped Annie get free, then led her out of the woods and headed her up the hill to where Danny was waiting. Then she whirled around, ready to stand off the wolf. Whatever the cost, she would not let the timber wolf have her baby. If that ole wolf ate her baby girl, it would be over her dead body! Ole Lobo would have to kill her first.

Three

Eli the Elk

Back in the woods, ole Lobo was getting his wind back. He was up on his front legs, trying to drag his bottom half up. His back and his back legs hurt. Already, he was beginning to get sore. Annie's mama had hit him hard!

Lobo walked slowly at first, then gradually picked up speed. His nose was in the air, twitching, trying to pick up the antelope's scent. Thinking about having that tender little antelope for his supper made

that ole wolf's mouth start watering.
And thinking about eating made
Lobo run faster and faster. He was
almost to the hill, the hill where
Mama Antelope was prepared for a
standoff.

"Here he comes, Mama! Here he comes!" Danny yelled.

"I see him, too!" came from frightened Annie.

Mama said, "Stay behind me, you two. Don't move! Whatever you do, don't run in opposite directions. Divide and conquer—that's what wild animals do—divide and conquer. They like to get one antelope or deer, or whatever they're hunting, off by itself, away from the herd. It's much easier to catch that way."

The timber wolf had just reached the top of the hill when a huge elk came trotting across the field. When the elk saw ole Lobo, he slowed down, then stopped. He stood there a second, sizing up the situation. Eli saw Mama Antelope prepared to defend her babies, and he saw the timber wolf, ready to attack.

Eli raised his head, tossed it into the air a couple of times, then came thundering across the field toward Lobo, gradually picking up speed.

Lobo stood looking from little Annie to the huge, charging elk, then reluctantly turned and ran down the hill, back in the direction from which he had come. He hated to give up his supper, but there would be another day. There would be another time when that big elk wouldn't be around to protect that little antelope. And by that time, the little antelope would be bigger. She would have a little more meat on her bones. Lobo glanced back a couple of times with a promising glare at Annie. And of course, little Annie's mama saw and understood the look on Lobo's face.

When Lobo was completely out of sight, Mama Antelope turned her attention to Eli. "Thanks, Eli. I'm sure glad you came along when you did. I have been teaching my little ones a few lessons in survival. I think we'll go join the rest of the herd now. Have you seen them?"

Eli the Elk rippled his muscles. His massive frame seemed to move in waves. "They're on the south slope of the next hill, enjoying the sun and the fresh green grass. Be careful, Mrs. Antelope. I saw a young coyote lurking just down the hill." Then, true to his nature, Eli added as he turned to leave, "Looks to me like you shouldn't be here anyhow—off by yourself with these two young ones. I figured antelope to be smarter than this."

Mama Antelope thanked Eli again and, after he was out of earshot, said, "So! What I've heard about Eli the Elk is true. Did you two notice what Eli said to me? Eli is known as a *put-down*. No matter what anyone does or says, Eli thinks it could have been done better or said better. Don't be like Eli, Annie and Danny. Don't either of you ever put anyone down."

With a motherly look at Annie and Danny, Mama Antelope said, "Let's go, you two. We've had enough lessons for today." Danny fell in behind his mama, but Annie bounded off in another direction.

Mama raised her head and called, "Annie! Annie Antelope! Come back here!"

Mama Antelope looked at Danny. Danny smiled and said, "I know, Mama. Annie is a little ole optimist! Ain't she, Mama? Huh? Ain't she?"

"*Isn't* she, Danny. *Isn't* she," Mama Antelope corrected.

About that time, little Annie Antelope came bounding out of the woods ahead of them. Her eyes were shining, and she was out of breath. She had cut through the woods and had gotten ahead of her mama and Danny. Boy! She always had fun! Well, almost always!

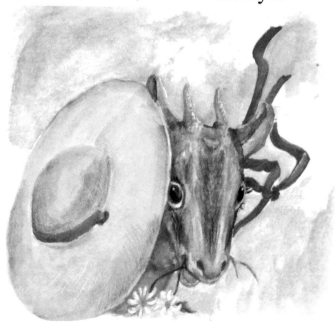

Four

Antelope Facts

The antelope family includes bison, buffalo, cattle, goats, and sheep. Although antelope resemble deer, they are much more closely related to cattle. Africa is the home of most antelope, although a few species survive in Asia, and a close relative, the mountain goat, lives in North America. Habitats most common to antelope are grasslands, dry plains, and forests. Some antelope live in swamplands, on hot deserts, or at high mountain elevations.

Antelope are ruminants, or cud chewers. They do not have incisors, or biting teeth, in the upper front jaw, and thus must tear off grass stems by exerting pressure with the lower teeth against the upper gum pad. This food is swallowed mainly unchewed and is later regurgitated from the stomach in small wads, or cuds, for thorough chewing with the molars.

chewing cud

Antelope have slender legs with two hoofed toes on each foot. Many of them have taller rumps than forequarters, with powerful rear leg muscles to facilitate running and leaping. Some can attain speeds of about thirty-five miles per hour. The rigid structure of the backbone enables them to run this fast and to jump high without injury to themselves. Their senses of smell and hearing are well developed, their vision less so.

The largest antelope, the giant eland of West Africa, may grow to a weight of more than 1,200 pounds and a shoulder height of six feet. The smallest, the royal antelope of Africa's western coastal regions, weighs about fifteen pounds and stands ten inches tall at the shoulder.

Most antelope have horns. Many horns are long and curved; some are ringed, and many are spiral, S-shaped, or lyre-shaped.

horns

The male four-horned antelope of Burma and India has two pairs of horns, one atop its head and the other on its forehead. Horns range in length from those of the royal antelope, which protrude less than one inch, to the corkscrew-shaped five foot horns of the kudu of eastern and southern Africa.

Antelope horns are nonbranching and have a bony core. They are not shed periodically, as are the antlers of deer but are permanent structures.

antelope

deer

The antelope group comprises more than one hundred species, including the gazelles. The North American pronghorn, often called pronghorn antelope, is not a true antelope.

Primitive antelope appeared in Eurasia in the late Miocene epoch, about twelve million years ago. Human-like apes, which evolved at about the same time, may have hunted antelope. Fossil remains found in East Africa give evidence that hominids hunted antelopes for food at least two million years ago.

Today farmers in sub-Saharan Africa manage herds of elands for milk production.